IGNITING VALUES

DORA D'COSTA

WORKBOOK PRESS LLC
187 E Warm Springs Rd,
Suite B285, Las Vegas, NV 89119, USA

Website: https://workbookpress.com/
Hotline: 1-888-818-4856
Email: admin@workbookpress.com

Ordering Information:
Quantity sales. Special discounts are available on quantity purchases by corporations, associations, and others.
For details, contact the publisher at the address above.

ISBN-13: 978-1-954753-09-9 (Paperback Version)
          978-1-954753-10-5 (Digital Version)

REV. DATE: 10/02/2021

Dora D'Costa

The best thing to give to your enemy is forgiveness; to an opponent, tolerance; to a friend, your heart; to your child, a good example; to a father, deference; to your mother, conduct that will make her proud of you; to yourself, respect; to all men, charity.

GOOD MANNERS

Thought: *Good manners will open doors that nothing else will.*

Theme: *Good manners enable us to live in harmony and it is appreciated at all times.*

Not far from where I lived there was a wonderful family that everyone admired. We got on very well and soon became very good friends. Just like my parents, Jane's and Isidore's parents had taught them to behave well and use their good manners intelligently.

My mother always said, "You lose nothing by using kind words" or saying "Thank you", "Please", "I beg your pardon" or "just being polite". It takes you far. "Good manners depict your soul".

Dad and Mum were good role models and it was easy to follow their footsteps. Mum often said, "It cost nothing to use your good manners. It can win you lots of friends". When we went to school it was good to enjoy

Jane's and Isidore's company as they belonged to our way of life. We were on the same plane and of like minds.

It was fun to have like minds work and play together. The values our parents taught us were put into practice in our day to day lives. Most of our friends fell into the same category. As dad would say, "Birds of the same feathers flock together".

What a pity it was to see some other children choose the wrong path and act nastily towards their peers. What goes around comes around. They were met with similar fights, rude words and sometimes nobody wanted to play with them. They were not ready to give up their bad ways for better things. They envied the good and inspiring girls and boys, who handled most issues very well. Jealousy crept in and they began to bully the ones who walked the straight path.

Something had to be done to bring about peace in the classroom, school and neighbourhood. Jane came up with the idea that we have two boxes: one for "good deeds" and the other, "I forgot about good deeds".

All we had to do is write our name and drop it into the respective box.

It didn't take long for all to begin using the "good deeds" box. Many had their names more often than others but it made us all work towards the same goal.

The classroom, school and neighbourhood had better people living in a friendly and cordial community. What a happy community it was!

Our parents are our first teachers!

Great parents are to be praised for their wonderful parenting.

Good manners
and
kindness
is always in fashion.

When one says
Thank You
It is more than good manners,
For it is the Soul that speaks.

The children of today
need to experience good manners in
their daily lives.
People around them should be their
role models.

EFFORT AND PERSISTENCE

Thought: *Set your mind on it, persist on working for it and you will be the winner!*

Theme: *Every effort you make and the more persistence you show in pursuing your goal, will bring home great returns.*

Jack admired his sister playing the piano with ease and proper timing. At gatherings Mary was always requested to play several pieces for the special listeners. All who heard her marvelled at her skill, accuracy and ease.

One sunny afternoon while the family was dining, Jack seemed to be in dream land. He seemed to be far away with his world wind thoughts. Mr. Smith awakened him from his world. "Hey Jack, what's the matter? You haven't answered my question." Jack was taken aback. "What is it, dad?"

"Didn't you hear me?" questioned his father.

Jack then admitted that he was thinking of learning how to play the guitar. As he was focussed on his thoughts, he missed out on his father's question.

"Never mind," said his understanding father. "So, tell me what prompted you to decide on learning the guitar?"

"I thought Mary and I could make a duo."

Mr. Smith thought it was a wonderful idea for his two children to work together as a musical team. It was agreed that Jack pursue his dream.

Mary and Jack were to go to the same musical centre to learn. Mary reminded Jack that he had to have his mind set on his goal, work hard and practice regularly.

"Thanks sis! I will do so!" was his reply. As days went by, Jack felt it was a lot of work. "Practice makes one perfect!" yelled Mary from the passage.

Months later, Jack realised what his mother had told him. "You have a goal. Now set your mind on it. Put in all the effort you can if you want your dreams to come true. No pain, no gain!"

He had received all the support possible from his family. It was left to him to do the rest.

Perseverance! That's the word. You sow tears to reap joy. Jack finally made it to success. His hard work paid him dividends. His mother and father sang while Mary played the piano and he the guitar. They were called "The Musical Family."

> *Every effort is a step forward to gain reward.*
>
> *Try and try until you succeed.*

YOU REAP WHAT YOU SOW.

WITH EFFORT YOU GAIN ACHIEVEMENT. WITH ACHIEVEMENT YOU GAIN HAPPINESS. WITH HAPPINESS YOU CAN CHANGE THE WORLD.

It was Christmas time and the dogs each got a toy. Louie was covered with white fur and received a white Christmas toy while Tugger had a lovely ginger and brown coat and had a toy that was brown. Both were very happy at the beginning and eager to play.

Soon Louie gave up competing. Tugger was playful and loved to tug at his toy. It gave him great joy to hear the tune of Jingle Bells.

Very soon we were tired of hearing the tune and placed his toy on the wine rack. Tugger was determined to get it back and have some fun. He jumped several times and finally succeeded in pulling it down. It was a lot of struggle; balancing, keeping steady, using one paw and his teeth but finally he learnt the art of retrieving it from the rack.

We all admired the dog's persistence and he taught us a lesson of how to strive for the thing we love.

Many of life's failures are people who did not realize how close they were to success when they gave up.

No one succeeds without effort… Those who succeed owe their success to perseverance.

Every time you fall stand up and begin again until you succeed.

HONESTY

Thought: *Honesty is the best policy.*

Theme: *Truth is an important virtue that is to be treasured.*

Long ago there were ladybirds that looked around for a leader. One bright sunny day they decided to set out for greener pastures and came to a common consensus to select a leader.

Without much ado they came upon a plan. They would set out one at a time to find out this beautiful land which they would inhabit. Each one of them would go his different path and return to where he started from with the information he gathered. Since there were five of them, one chose to go Northwards, the other walked towards the South, another to the West, the fourth to the East and the fifth ladybird stood at the commencing point. The lady bird that went towards the North returned fast and described the land as beautiful, full of green pastures with a spread of wild flowers of different hues and above all a lake with fresh clear water.

The ladybird that went eastwards returned with news that it was a huge stretch of land that was covered with red mud and very dry. There was absolutely no water and it would be difficult to live there.

Soon the ladybird that went in the westerly direction brought good tidings that the land was rich and gorgeous and they all would love to inhabit it.

Finally the last ladybird returned after a very long period to complain that he could find no water, the land was soggy from a flood and they would not be able to live in such a marshy land.

The ladybird that stood waiting for the four to return was patient and wondered why three of his mates took less time to get back whilst the last mate to return had taken ages to get back. They each gave their commentary on their research of the land. It was discovered that the last ladybird was honest and did his best to discover the truth of the place he went to. He left no stone unturned, was precise and painted the picture accurately.

Obviously he was chosen to be the leader. The others had a spot painted on their backs for the lie they told.

Are you one of those who would like to be labelled the same way?

"HONESTY IS VALUED BY ALL, AND WHEN WE ARE DISHONEST, PEOPLE LOSE FAITH IN US."

RESPECT

Thought: *Respect yourself and you will find that others will respect you.*

Theme: *Respect is when you care about others' feelings before you act, do or say something.*

Tommy walked into class everyday with an attitude, thinking he was superior to others. He would grab other students' things and throw them about. Most of the students showed patience and tolerance. They put up with his rude behaviour. When they realised that he would not stop, they approached him and asked him to use better sense and treat them with respect. Tommy promised he would. A few students warned Tommy that they would report him to the teacher.

The very next day he was in a group that were building a house with blocks. Tommy chose to kick the blocks that were set up. This angered the boys and they told him it was not right for him to do what he did.

He was reported to the teacher. Tommy was called to give an account of what he had done. He said it was a mistake and he wouldn't repeat it again.

Tommy was given three chances to prove that he could make a change for the better. He continued in the same old way and got himself into trouble.

Finally his parents were called and informed of his mean behaviour. Tommy promised to change. He was reminded of the golden rule that he had to treat others as he would want them to treat him. Tommy kept to his word and all noticed the change in him. He soon had many friends because of his good ways. They were drawn to him as bees are drawn to honey. He learnt what true friendship is.

Tommy learnt that in order to gain respect he had to first respect himself and then show respect to others.

*The most beautiful people on earth
are those who respect themselves first
and are then able to respect others.*

Show Respect to gain Respect.

*Respect is earned
Honesty is appreciated
Trust is gained
Loyalty is returned.*

FRIENDLINESS

Thought: *To have a friend is to be a friend.*

Theme: *Friends accept each other for what they are.*

Raymond woke up early every day to feed his pets. He loved nurturing them and then he would prepare to go to school. All at home appreciated his love for his pets and the devotion shown to them.

In school he was a different person. He was very unkind and aggressive. Many times he wanted his own way. John was his good friend who often stood up to him and told him it wasn't the right way to go about in life. "You reap what you sow". Raymond didn't pay heed to the friendly advice.

John stood by him through thick and thin. Whenever he got into trouble John was there for him; talking convincingly and making him understand that what he was doing was not going to be tolerated for long.

Raymond realised he was losing his friends and they did not wish to play or hang around with him. John was his stalwart friend who guided him on the right path. He realised there was something good in Raymond when he overnighted at his place and realised the love he had for his pets. He got Raymond to transfer this love to his friends.

Not very long after there was a change of heart and Raymond turned out to be a good leader who led the path to progress and become an achiever.

John left an indelible stamp on Raymond's heart.

Good friends are hard to find, harder to leave and impossible to forget.

A friend is someone who knows all about you

Friends are angels that lift us to our feet
When our wings have trouble
Remembering how to fly.

Friendship
is not about whom
you have known
the longest; it is about
who came and never left
your side.

There are some people
in life that make you
laugh a little louder,
smile a little bigger and
live life just a little better.

Best Friends

Fight for you
Respect you
Include you
Encourage you
Need you
Dote on you
Stand by you.

Good friends
bring out the
best in you.

Responsibility

Thought: *Great people are responsible people who do whatever they do as well as they can.*

Theme: *You and only you are responsible for every decision and choice you make.*

RESPONSIBILITY

Responsibility is doing my job to the best of
my ability.
Responsibility is caring for others.
Responsibility is giving it my best.
Responsibility is doing my share of the work.
Responsibility is taking good care of things.
Responsibility is helping others when they are
in need.
Responsibility is being fair to everyone.
Responsibility is working well as a team.
Responsibility is helping to make a better
world.

Responsible people make the world a better place.

At the beginning of each scholastic year, the teacher prepared a duty chart of tasks that the children are capable of doing. Each child opts for what they would like to do. Some of the tasks were: class captain, switching on or off the lights, library monitor, collecting notices from the teacher's tub, putting the books in the classroom in order, seeing to the cleanliness of the class and so on. These duties when taken on, help inculcate the value of being responsible.

It is amazing to see that some take on the job very seriously and give their best. Others will do it occasionally and a few will forget conveniently.

Mary Smith was voted class captain. She was one of those who took her job very conscientiously and gave it her best. Her motto was: 'Whatever you do, do it well'. She was also able to help others in their tasks when possible. All loved her and she was every teacher's and student's favourite.

Mary was a wonderful role model and her peers adored her. At the end of the year she was voted, 'Best student of the year'.

It pays to be different, hardworking and dutiful.

Responsibility is the key to a person's good will and maturity.

We all have a right to be a good individual and also obligated to be one.

Cooperation

Thought: *Working together in a team brings forth great achievements.*

Theme: *Each individual needs to be*
Responsible
Committed
Co-operative.

In a good working classroom everyone is happy and succeeds. This was brought to light when students worked as a team.

At first some students did not cooperate while some others worked independently and in a responsible manner. They vied with one another to be successful as individuals. In these cases duties were completed. The others took things with a pinch of salt.

When opportunities arose for the students to work in teams, one could see that each was responsible to give their best, cooperate and be committed as a team member. All tasks were completed in less than the expected time.

It could be concluded that many hands make light work. Together we can stand united. Divided we fall.

Are you the person who is responsible, committed and cooperative?

All continents put together form the world.

The most complex tasks and assignments can be made simpler when we focus together on the solutions.

UNITED WE STAND DIVIDED WE FALL.

Working together is an art and an individual's personal gift.

Acceptance

Thought: *Life is made of choices: you either accept things as they are, or you take on the responsibility of changing them for the better.*

Theme: *To learn to accept each other's faults and choose to celebrate each other's differences. It is one of the most important keys to creating a healthy growing and lasting relationship.*

THE WORLD TODAY

Romans 15:7 *"Accept one another, then, just as Christ accepted you, in order to bring praise to God."*

We live in a multicultural society where we are of different colour, culture and follow diverse customs and religions. People in our society view things from their own perspective, attempt a variety of plans and in short follow varied paths to achieve what they desire to gain happiness.

Each and every one of us has the responsibility to accept others just as they are: ***a creation of the Creator.***

Ephesians 4:2-3: *"Be completely humble and gentle; be patient, bearing with one another in love. Make every effort to keep the unity of the Spirit through the bond of peace."*

Through acceptance we embrace whatever we have (the whole package). Holding it like a glass bowl we discover the fragility of glass and we discover positive experiences and feelings that enable us to find love, peace and joy. We need to be able to discern what needs to be changed and what is to be accepted. The prayer of St. Francis of Assisi says it all:

God, grant me the serenity
to accept the things I cannot change
courage to change the things I can
and wisdom
to know the difference.

If we are able to accept ourselves with all our imperfections and great qualities, we can accept others as they are. It enables us to look up to ourselves and not just trust and have confidence in ourselves but also to accept others in the same way.

Acceptance leads us to celebrate our strengths and those of others thus creating a safe place for ourselves and others to live in. Our world is a better place because of our insights, understanding and love which enables us to grow into the best human beings we can be. What a wonderful world it will be!

I am reminded of a story!

William was a wonderful husband to Mary and a loving father of David. Their lives were simple and they enjoyed one another's company more than anything.

> *Accept what is,*
> *let go of what was*
> *and have faith*
> *In what will be.*

As time went by Mary got sick and died. William and David missed her a lot. William gave his son whatever he could.

David grew up to be a man and married Ann. He worked hard and was well known, respected and loved in his town. William, being the generous man he was, allowed David and his wife to live with him under the same roof.

Years passed by and William grew old and weak. David had a son who simply loved his grandfather who was always there for him. One day William not only dropped food on the table but also broke the plate he ate from. David was unforgiving, gave his father a plastic plate and sat him in a corner. The old man said not a word.

The young boy who adored his grandfather could not bear to see him being treated so. He decided to make a wooden plate. David noticed his son at work and inquired what he was up to. He was informed that a wooden bowl was being made for him which he could use when he grew old. It dawned on David how he had treated his father. William was called back to the table where he belonged.

The golden rule is: **"Do to others what you would have them do to you."**

> *When you accept yourself, you will be able to accept others and the whole world will accept you.*

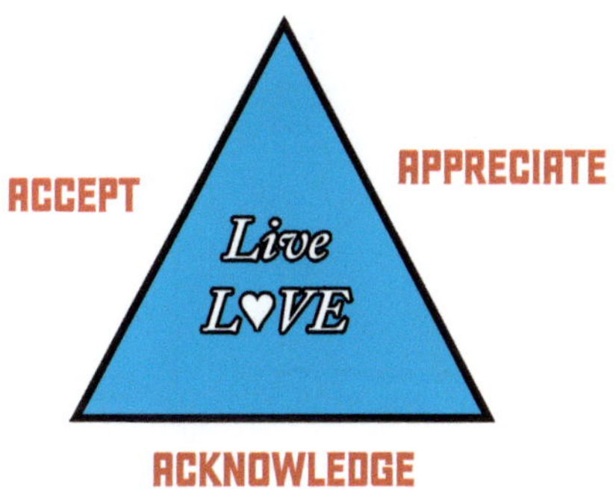

> *Life is made of choices:*
> *To accept things as they do exist or take*
> *on the responsibility and accept to change*
> *them.*

Accept one another, then just as **Christ** *has accepted you, in order to bring praise to* **God.** *Romans15:7*

There's a story behind every person. There's a reason why they are the way they are. Think about that before you judge someone.